My Little Golden Word Book

Originally published under the title *Things in My House*.

By Joe Kaufman

A GOLDEN BOOK • NEW YORK
Western Publishing Company, Inc., Racine, Wisconsin 53404

There are all kinds
of things in my house:

a hammer,

a shoe,

a pencil,

a sock,

an apple,

a flower,

a fork,

and a clock.

A saw,

a leaf,

a ball,

a bat,

an umbrella,

glasses,

a block,

and a hat.

A kettle,

a lemon,

a glove,

a toy boat,

a toothbrush,

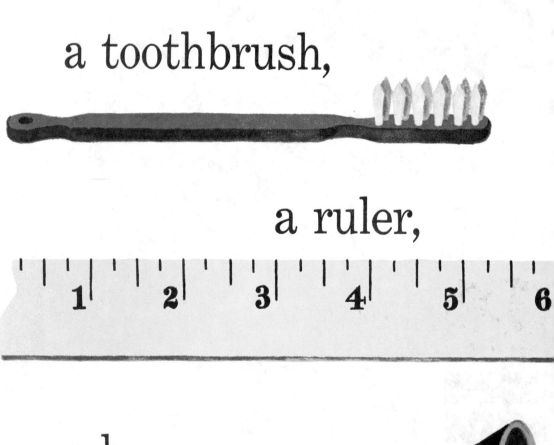

a ruler,

a horn,

and  a coat.

A candle,

a doll,

a cookie,

a nail,

a locomotive,

an onion,

a shovel,  and a pail.

A fireman's hat,

a walnut,

a lamp,

scissors,

a cup,

a brush,

and a stamp.

An airplane,

a puppet,

an orange,

a spoon,

a window,

and outside...
stars and the moon.